Unknown

Colin Thompson

illustrations by Anna Pignataro

Walker & Company
New York

The noise was deafening.

Twenty dogs were shouting

at the tops of their voices.

Me
me
me
me
me
choose me.

The little dog in the last cage was too scared to shout. She just sat at the back of her cage and shivered.

In the next cage the biggest, wildest dog she'd ever seen in her life leaped at the fence, foaming at the mouth.

"OVER HERE!"

he shouted at the humans.

"OVER HERE! I'M A <u>REAL</u> DOG."

The caretaker put a sign on each cage in the animal shelter to tell the humans about the dog inside. There was Stray and next to him, Owner-Died and Owner-Gone-Abroad. Another was called Unwanted-Christmas-Gift.

6

The huge dog was called Grown-Too-Large. And the little dog in the last cage was called Unknown because she'd been left in a box outside the shelter in the middle of the night.

"Hey, take me!" shouted Grown-Too-Large. "Or I'll bite you."

The humans passed each cage, shaking their heads, and then they left. Gradually the barking died down

and the dogs grew sad and tired. They curled up in their boxes and went to sleep.

It was the same every day, over and over again.
Sometimes the dogs were taken out of their cages
and walked up and down, and sometimes dogs went
off to new homes. When they did, there were always
other unwanted dogs to take their places.

People with children took the puppies and friendly dogs
home to play ball in the backyard and to curl up
together to watch television. Little old ladies took little
old dogs home to keep them company in the long

afternoons, to sit on their laps and dream and eat meat and potatoes and cake on Fridays. It seemed that for every type of dog there was the right type of person—big dog and big person, small dog and small person.

All except for Grown-Too-Large, who was so ferocious no one would go near him, and Unknown. No one seemed to notice her. The other dogs ran forward, barking and wagging their tails, but Unknown was too nervous and sat in her bed in the shadows. She was the same colors as the shadows so most people looking into her cage thought it was empty and kept on walking.

One night the skies grew wild. Angry rain threw itself on the tin roofs of the cages, drumming like wild horses. It poured onto the concrete like a great waterfall while lightning flashed over the trees across the yard. Unable to sleep with the noise,

the dogs sat in their cages watching the storm as they waited for it to pass. Unknown liked the rain. It washed the dust off the world and made everything smell fresh and alive. But the smells—the warm earth, the clean leaves—made her feel lonely.

In the back of his cage, big and savage Grown-Too-Large shook like a leaf.

With every crack of lightning he shivered more. He put his paws over his head and tried to shut everything out. There were two blinding flashes and suddenly the trees were on fire. The rain slowed to a drizzle as the flames danced through the branches, leaping from tree to tree until the yard and its row of cages were surrounded by a ring of fire. The big dog was scared out of his wits, but there was nowhere to hide.

"We're all going to die!" cried Grown-Too-Large at the top of his voice, as burning branches began to fall down around them. "Help! Help! Somebody Help!" But even his loudest barks were lost in the thunder and lightning.

Unknown could see that no one was going to come. Who would be out on a night like this?

She knew that if something were to be done, she would have to do it herself. So she scratched at the wire in the darkest corner of her cage. It was getting very hot. In some places the wire walls of the cages were beginning to glow. Unknown's paws were split and bleeding, but at last she made a hole just big enough to squeeze through, and she ran through the rain of burning leaves until she was outside the ring of trees.

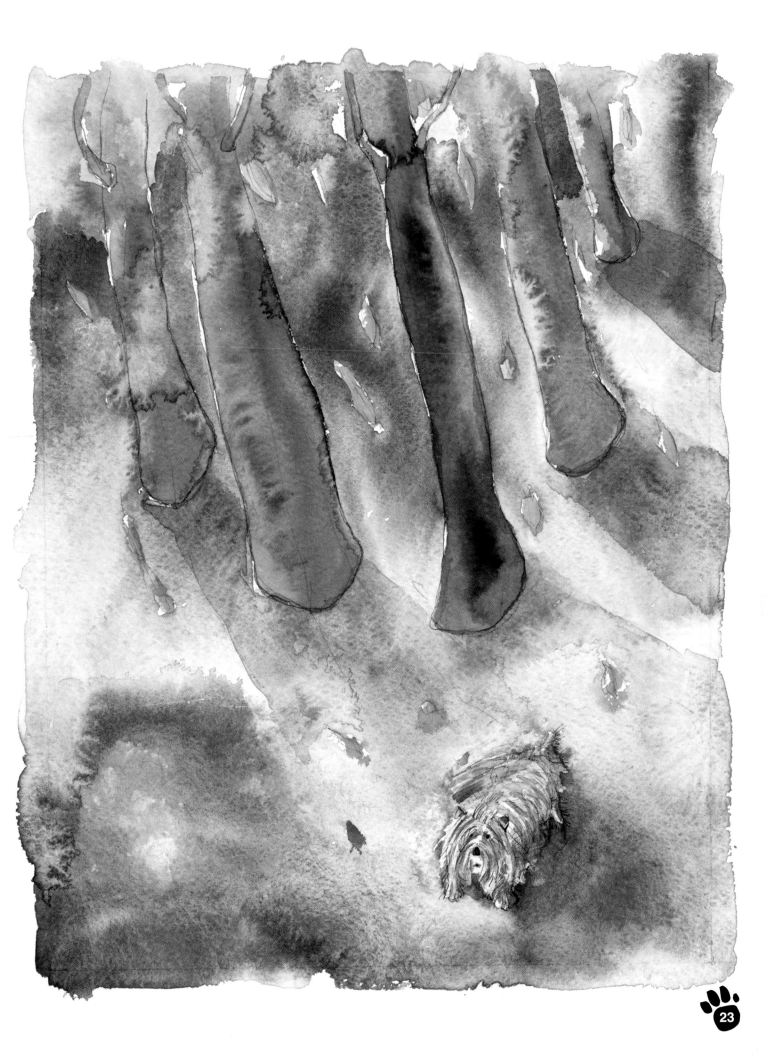

Unknown ran to a house across the road and barked at the top of her voice at the front door. At last someone looked out. It was the caretaker of the shelter and he recognized Unknown immediately. Unknown ran back across the road, followed by the caretaker and his wife, who raced along opening the cages and leading the dogs to safety. They all ran through the burning trees toward the house. All except Grown-Too-Large, who was too scared to move and had to be carried like a baby over the road. Only one dog, Keeps-Running-Off, ran away.

"He'll be back," said the caretaker, wrapping Grown-Too-Large's head in a wet towel.

"He's here about four times a year. He's had more
owners than I can remember."

The next day, Unknown's picture was on the front page of the newspaper. Suddenly there were about two hundred families who wanted to give her a home.

"I got lucky. But it would be good," she said to Grown-Too-Large, as she left the animal shelter with her new, loving family, "if we could put all the humans in cages and walk along with our noses in the air and choose the ones WE wanted."

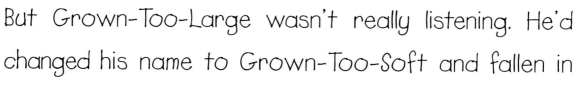

But Grown-Too-Large wasn't really listening. He'd changed his name to Grown-Too-Soft and fallen in

love with the caretaker and his wife and their five children and their other dog and their cat and their hamster, Nigel.

For Anne
CT
For my sister Rose, and for Niki, Timmy, Caesar, and Otto
AP

Text copyright © 2000 by Colin Thompson
Illustrations copyright © 2000 by Anna Pignataro

First published in the United States of America in 2000 by
Walker Publishing Company, Inc.

Published in association with Hodder Headline Australia Pty Limited
(A member of the Hodder Headline Group)
Level 22, 201 Kent Street, Sydney NSW 2000

Library of Congress Cataloging-in-Publication Data
Thompson, Colin (Colin Edward)
Unknown /Colin Thompson ; illustrations by Anna Pignataro.
p. cm.
Summary: Ignored by prospective human owners who walk past her cage at the pound,
a shy dog with an unusual name becomes a hero during a lightning storm.
ISBN 0-8027-8730-4—ISBN 0-8027-8731-2 (lib. bdg.)
[1. Dogs— Fiction. 2. Animals— Treatment— Fiction.] I. Pignataro, Anna, 1965- ill.
II. Title.

PZ7.T371424 Un 2000
[E]—dc21   99-057123
Illustration technique: Watercolor and ink
Design concept by Susie Agoston O'Connor
Printed in Hong Kong

2 4 6 8 10 9 7 5 3 1

Visit Colin Thompson's homepage at
http://www.atlantis.aust.com/~colinet
or e-mail him on colinet@atlantis.aust.com